"HELLO READING books are a perfect introduction to reading. Brief sentences full of word repetition and full-color pictures stress visual clues to help a child take the first important steps toward reading. Mastering these story books will build children's reading confidence and give them the enthusiasm to stand on their own in the world of words."

—Bee Cullinan
Past President of the International Reading
Association, Professor in New York University's
Early Childhood and Elementary Education Program

"Readers aren't born, they're made. Desire is planted—planted by parents who work at it."

—Jim Trelease
author of *The Read Aloud Handbook*

"When I was a classroom reading teacher, I recognized the importance of good stories in making children understand that reading is more than just recognizing words. I saw that children who have ready access to story books get excited about reading. They also make noticeably greater gains in reading comprehension. The development of the HELLO READING stories grows out of this experience."

—Harriet Ziefert
M.A.T., New York University School of Education
Author, Language Arts Module,
Scholastic Early Childhood Program

For Jamie, again

For Jon, again

VIKING KESTREL
Viking Penguin Inc., 40 West 23rd Street, New York, New York 10010, U.S.A.
Penguin Books Ltd, 27 Wrights Lane, London W8 5TZ (Publishing & Editorial) and
Harmondsworth, Middlesex, England (Distribution & Warehouse)
Penguin Books Australia Ltd., Ringwood, Victoria, Australia
Penguin Books Canada Limited, 2801 John St., Markham, Ontario, Canada L3R 1B4
Penguin Books (N.Z.) Ltd, 182–190 Wairau Road, Auckland 10, New Zealand

1   2   3   4   5   92   91   90   89   88

Library of Congress Cataloging-in-Publication Data
Ziefert, Harriet.
Andy toots his horn.
(Hello reading! ; 10)
Summary: Andy bothers everyone in his house when he toots his horn,
but when he wanders outside, everyone misses him and the noise he makes.
[1. Noise—Fiction]   I. Hoffman, Sanford, ill.   II. Title.   III. Series: Ziefert, Harriet.
Hello reading! ; 10.
PZ7.Z478An   1988b   [E]   87-25339
ISBN 0-670-82035-0

Andy Toots His Horn

Harriet Ziefert
Pictures by Sanford Hoffman

VIKING KESTREL

Andy wanted to make noise.
So he went to his room
and found his red horn.

Andy tooted his horn.
Toot toot!
Toot toot toot!

Andy's grandpa said,
"Don't toot here!
I'm eating."

Andy's grandma said,
"Don't toot here!
I'm reading."

"Don't toot here,"
said Andy's mom.
"You'll scare the cat."

Andy was mad.
He threw his horn and said,
"I can't toot near Grandma!
I can't toot near Grandpa!
I can't toot near Mom and Dad!
I can't toot near the cat!
So where can I toot?"

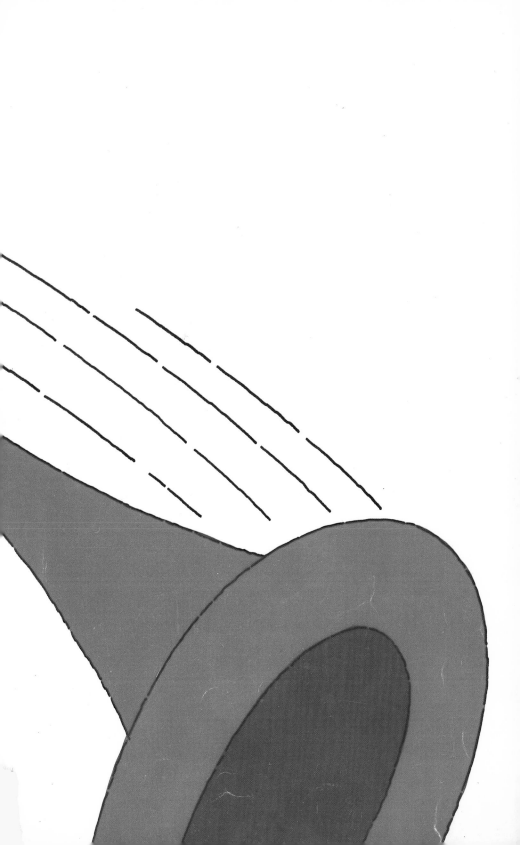

Andy grabbed his horn
and ran to his room.
He shut the door and
tooted as loud as he could.

Andy made a big noise.
But it was no fun.
No one could hear his music.

Andy went outside.
He wet his lips.
Then he tooted
as loud as he could.

A cat heard Andy's toot.

A dog heard him, too.

A little girl heard Andy.

And so did a little boy.

Andy saw the cat, and the dog,
and the girl, and the boy.
He said, "I'll be the band leader.
You be the band."

They marched all the way
to Andy's house.

"Where have you been?"
asked Andy's mom and dad.

"I missed you,"
said Andy's grandma.

"We all missed you,"
said Andy's grandpa.
"It gets too quiet
when you are not here."

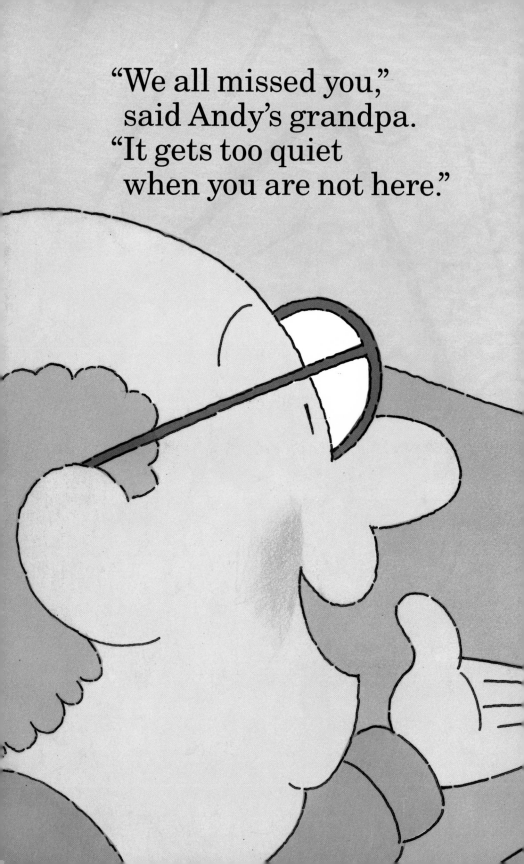

"Too quiet?" said Andy.
"I'll make some noise."
So Andy tooted his horn.
Toot toot!
Toot toot toot!